S0-EIH-978

Western Wagon Trains

Tim McNeese

Crestwood House
New York

Maxwell Macmillan Canada
Toronto

Maxwell Macmillan International
New York Oxford Singapore Sydney

Design: Deborah Fillion
Illustrations: © Chris Duke

Crestwood House
Macmillan Publishing Company
866 Third Avenue
New York, NY 10022

Maxwell Macmillan Canada, Inc.
1200 Eglinton Avenue East
Suite 200
Don Mills, Ontario M3C 3N1

Macmillan Publishing Company is part of the
Maxwell Communication Group of Companies

First Edition

Printed in the United States of America

10 9 8 7 6 5 4 3 2 1

Library of Congress Cataloging-in-Publication Data

McNeese, Tim.
Western wagon trains / by Tim McNeese. — 1st ed.
p. cm. — (Americans on the move)
Summary: Describes the western migration along the Oregon and California Trails during the nineteenth century.
ISBN 0-89686-734-X
1. West (U.S.)—Description and travel—To 1848—Juvenile literature. 2. West (U.S.)—Description and travel—1848-1860—Juvenile literature. 3. Overland journeys to the Pacific—Juvenile literature. 4. Frontier and pioneer life—West (U.S.)—Juvenile literature. 5. Pioneers—Travel—West (U.S.)—History—19th century—Juvenile literature. 6. Oregon Trail—Juvenile literature. 7. California Trail—Juvenile literature. [1. West (U.S.)—Description and travel—To 1848. 2. West (U.S.)—Description and travel—1848-1860. 3. Overland journeys to the Pacific. 4. Frontier and pioneer life—West (U.S.) 5. Oregon Trail. 6. California Trail.] I. Title. II. Series: McNeese, Tim. Americans on the move.
F592.M36 1993
917.804'2—dc20 91-42076

★

Contents

During the early 1800s American pioneers set out to expand their small nation. Their travels were an exciting part of American history.

Introduction

Today the United States stretches from the Atlantic Ocean to the Pacific Ocean and beyond. But during most of America's early history, the nation was much smaller. The original 13 colonies ran along the Atlantic seaboard from Massachusetts to Georgia. Throughout the 1700s, tens of thousands of settlers moved over the Appalachian Mountains into the Ohio River valley. These pioneers settled the lands west to the Mississippi River. After the American Revolution, the Mississippi River became the western boundary of the new United States.

But it would not be long before colonial Americans looked to the land west of the Mississippi. From 1804 through 1806, explorers Meriwether Lewis and William Clark traveled up the Missouri River and crossed the Rocky Mountains. They went all the way to the **Oregon Country,** today the states of Oregon and Washington. Their reports encouraged a new breed of American called the **mountain man.** These hardy people went west to trap beaver and other furbearers. The success of these trappers encouraged pioneers to head west in covered wagons from the 1830s through the 1850s. During the migration's peak year—1850—approximately 55,000 emigrants rolled their wagons west along the **Oregon Trail.** By 1869, when the transcontinental railroad across the west was completed, at least 350,000 pioneers had traveled along the now-famous route. Those who emigrated along the California Trail, which branched off the Oregon Trail, panned for gold and began farms in the late 1840s and the 1850s. The story of these early migrants' determination to make a new home in the great, untamed western lands is an exciting one that is full of adventure.

Lewis and Clark explored western areas with the help of their native American guide Sacagawea.

Establishing the Oregon Trail

The first people on the Oregon Trail did not travel by wagon. The earliest travelers were the native Americans. They had established many footpaths across the land that would one day become the United States. These paths were used by the mountain women and men. One of the first mountain people to walk the Oregon Trail was a trapper named Robert Stuart. In 1811 Stuart and a group of trappers sailed around South America and landed at the mouth of the Columbia River. This river flows from the Rockies to the Pacific Ocean. Here Stuart founded a trading post which he called **Astoria.** (Stuart and his crew worked for a man named John Jacob Astor.)

One day the expedition's ship exploded and was destroyed. This left the trappers stranded, with no way to report back east to Astor. Luckily, a second group of Astor's crew just happened to find the Astoria encampment. This group had traveled overland across the Rocky Mountains and had floated down the Columbia River.

The two groups decided that the only way to report to Astor was to travel back over the Rockies and across the western lands to the East. In June 1812 Robert Stuart led a group from Astoria up the Columbia River. The group was first helped by friendly Indians. But in the Rockies, unfriendly native Americans stole their horses. This left the tiny group unsure how to get across the Rocky Mountains.

On October 22, 1812, Stuart and his followers found a way through the great mountain range. The pass was at the south end of the Wind River range, in what is today Wyoming. The group noted that the gap in the mountains was wide enough for wagons to pass through. In later years, the range was called **South Pass.** It was through this pass that tens of thousands of migrants and their wagons would conquer the Rockies

on their trips west along the Oregon Trail. By March 1813 Stuart and his party reached St. Louis, Missouri. He did not realize it at the time, but Stuart had established the route of what came to be called the Oregon Trail.

First Wagons on the Oregon Trail

For years the Oregon Trail was used by fur trappers and traders. But these people did not travel the trail in wagons. They used pack mules from Missouri to carry their furs and supplies.

The first wagons traveled the Oregon Trail in 1830. That year three mountain men—Jedediah Smith, David E. Jackson and William Sublette—took ten wagons from St. Louis to the eastern side of the Rocky

Friendly native Americans guided Stuart's group through part of their journey.

Early wagons on the Oregon Trail were built to carry heavy loads of goods for trading.

Mountains. Their wagons were loaded with supplies for western fur trappers. These three men had formed the Rocky Mountain Fur Company. They traded their goods with western trappers at a **rendezvous,** an annual event throughout the 1830s, where trappers brought the season's catch and traded with entrepreneurs for new traps, tobacco, gunpowder and whiskey. These wagons of the Rocky Mountain Fur Company were the first to travel the Oregon Trail. And while the group had not taken their wagons west over the mountains to the Oregon Country, they were certain that it could be done.

During the 1830s westerners made advances in wagon travel along the Oregon Trail. In 1836 a missionary party joined a trapper party traveling along the trail by wagon. The trapper group was led by Smith, Jackson and Sublette. The missionary group included Marcus Whitman, a Presbyterian minister, and Samual Parker, a Congregationalist minister, and their wives. The fur company had seven wagons and a cart which were pulled by teams of six mules. The missionaries had two wagons of their own. Whitman and Parker were headed to Oregon to preach Christianity to the Indians. The trip took the missionaries across the endless plains of today's Kansas and Nebraska. Whitman's wife, Narcissa, kept a diary of her travels. She wrote about the difficulty of the trip. Concerning the food, she wrote: "I can scarce eat [dried buffalo strips], it appears so filthy, but it will keep us alive and we ought to be thankful for it."

On September 1, 1836, the Whitmans and their party arrived at a fur-trading outpost near modern-day Walla Walla, Washington. The missionaries were forced to abandon their wagons, which had broken down by that time. Still, the missionary group had achieved something important through their travels. They had proved that women of European heritage could travel the Oregon Trail and survive. Many mountain men of the day were certain that such a trip was too difficult for the strongest woman. Narcissa Whitman and the other missionary woman were the first Euramerican women to travel the trail and cross through the Rockies and beyond.

Other women soon followed. In 1840, two mountain couples discovered the Whitman wagons and repaired them. They then took them across the Blue Mountains all the way to Oregon.

Then came the first overland emigrant wagon train to make the entire trip from Missouri to Oregon and California. The group was led by a young Missouri schoolteacher named John Bidwell. He had never been on the Oregon Trail before but was eager to make his fortune out west. He signed up 500 other Missourians to follow him along the trail. But when the spring of 1841 came around, only a handful of emigrants showed up for the trip. Many had been discouraged from going west by stories they were hearing from those who had started the trip along the trail, only to return in failure.

Despite the poor turnout of followers, Bidwell was determined to go. Sixty-nine men, women and children decided to follow him. The group was very poor, having only $100 cash among them. Some drove ox-drawn wagons; some were in carriages. Still others were on horseback. Many in the group did not know whether they wanted to go to Oregon or California. The group set out for the trail completely unprepared for the long, difficult trip ahead.

Bidwell's group was lucky enough to connect with a mountain man named Tom Fitzpatrick, who led them over part of the trail. But the group did not get

Members of western wagon-train parties traveled together for safety during their long and difficult journey.

along well. By the time they arrived at the South Pass, some people in the group decided to go to Oregon with Fitzpatrick. The rest, led by Bidwell, headed south for California. Fitzpatrick could give his group only the simplest directions.

The Bidwell group—33 men, 1 woman and a child—had a very difficult journey. They wandered across the deserts and mountains. They were often far from any actual trail. When their animals became too weak to pull heavy loads, the party was forced to leave their wagons behind. The group ate horse and ox meat to keep from starving. By sheer determination and luck, John Bidwell and his followers finally made their way to the San Joaquin River valley in California.

The next year a member of the Bidwell party went back to Missouri to lead another group of western travelers to California. Word of the success of the Bidwell group and others spread fast. The mass western migration of hundreds of thousands of settlers was about to begin. In 1842, 200 emigrants went west along the trail. The next year was the time of the **great migration,** when over 1,000 pioneers pushed their way across the prairies. Many traveled in a great train of 120 wagons. Marcus Whitman, the missionary, was their leader. This group numbered 875 men, women and children. The party made their way to the Willamette River valley in Oregon. The Oregon Country soon saw other, even larger, groups arrive in this great western "promised land."

Traveling West on the Oregon Trail

The trip from Independence, Missouri, to the Willamette River valley in Oregon was about 2,000 miles. It was a difficult and dangerous six-month trip for human and beast. Many of the earlier wagon trains were ill prepared and ill equipped for such a lengthy trip. But soon the wagon trains became organized. While each trip for each train was different, a typical pattern developed for the Oregon Trail wagon trains.

Early wagon trains were made up of 25 to 30 families. Later trains sometimes had about 200. Each wagon train elected a captain who would lead the group and make important decisions. Larger wagon trains were divided into smaller groups with several captains. All members of a train agreed to a list of rules. Every person who could, signed the train rules. Those who broke the most serious rules were expelled from the group. Since no one wanted to be left in the wilderness alone, there were few problems between travelers on the trail. When an important decision needed to be made, the train's captain called a general council for a vote.

Captains often did not actually guide the group along the trail. In the early years, many wagon trains were led by mountain people who knew the trails well. Men such as Tom Fitzpatrick, Jim Bridger and Kit Carson found steady jobs as trail guides long after the western fur trade dried up.

Only the strongest animals could pull the heavily loaded wagons over long distances.

A New Kind of "Western Wagon"

The western trails caused a lot of wear and tear on the wagons the pioneers used. The trip took the emigrants over rugged land and mountainous passes. Travelers needed a wagon that could withstand the 2,000-mile trek. For many decades, pioneers and freighters east of the Mississippi River had relied on the large Conestoga wagons. These were heavy, boat-shaped wagons with great, billowing canvas covers.

But these wagons were too heavy for animals to pull over tall mountains, especially for 2,000 miles! A new wagon was designed for the western trails. Generally, the new wagon had a box measuring 10 feet long by 4 feet wide by 2 feet deep. The wagon weighed 1,000 pounds when empty and could carry between 1,000 and 1,500 pounds of household goods. The box was scoop-bottomed to help keep the wagon load from spilling out when traveling in the mountains. Before the travelers headed west, the wagons were caulked to keep the water out. Such wagons could float across rivers without getting the load wet. The weight carried was determined by the number of animals pulling the wagon. Back east, most wagons were pulled by horses, but the western wagons needed stronger stock. Typically, six oxen (three yoked pairs) were used. Some pioneers used six mules instead. Four oxen were enough to pull the average loaded wagon going west. The third pair were rotated in to relieve the others and give the oxen a needed rest. Oxen were used on western wagon trains for several reasons. They tended to be stronger than other animals, they would feed on prairie grass, they did not run away and thieves would not steal them as they did horses. Oxen were cheaper than horses or mules. They cost about $50 each, while mules ran about $90 apiece.

Family members cooperated in many tasks to make life on the trail run as efficiently as possible.

It was important to keep the livestock healthy on the trip across the western prairies and mountains. Animals could become overworked and unable to pull the wagons. Each day, around noon, the wagon trains stopped for several hours to give the oxen an opportunity to graze and rest. This slowed the trip, but, without such stops, the animals could not complete the journey.

Oxen could pull a loaded wagon at a speed of about 2 miles an hour on flat land. On most traveling days, a wagon train could cover about 15 miles. Some days, a train might advance 20 miles, while on others it would cover only 10 miles. Pioneers kept their wagon wheels well greased to give their oxen an easier time pulling. Good wheel maintenance was important while crossing the western territories.

A western wagon was called a **prairie schooner,** because its white canvas covering resembled a ship's sails. The cover was made of heavy, strong canvas or cotton twill. It was waterproofed with a treatment of **linseed oil.** Some pioneers sewed pockets on the insides of their wagons' canvas coverings. Wooden bows made of hickory held the cover up, allowing about 5 feet of headroom in a wagon bed. Pucker ropes at both ends were drawn together to keep out dust and give the pioneers some privacy at night.

These wagons were difficult to maneuver across the rugged western landscape. They were rarely balanced and could easily tip over. Heavy blocks, placed between the wagon bed and the axles, raised the bed up 18 inches to help keep out water when crossing rivers. But these blocks made the wagon top-heavy. Wagons then tipped over more easily. The weight in the wagons was never evenly distributed. When empty, the prairie schooner featured a toolbox on one side and sometimes a 40-gallon water barrel on the other. Even if the load inside was carefully packed to prevent it from sliding around, wagons were constantly falling over, especially when going uphill.

The ride on a covered wagon was generally rough. Few prairie schooners had springs or even brakes. Pioneers often dragged a log to slow a wagon when going downhill. Steering a wagon was difficult. When making a turn, the outside rear wheel turned at the same speed as the inner one even though it was covering more ground. As a result, the outer wheel would slide or skid until the turn was complete. Traveling even along the flat plains in waist-high prairie grass was a very bumpy ride!

Pioneers built their wagons out of hardwoods which could stand the daily abuse of western travel. Wagons were built by skilled workers who carefully put the wagon together with seasoned or kiln-dried hardwoods. Different woods were used for different parts of the wagon. The wheel hubs were often made from elm or Osage orange. Wheel spokes were cut from oak or hickory. The outer part of the wheel, called the felloe, was made of ash or beech. The wagon box was generally ash, while hickory was used for the wagon tongue. Sometimes pioneers took along replacement pieces for their wagons. When prairie schooners crossed the hot and dry plains, wagon parts would shrink, causing breakdowns.

Eating on the Trail

Most pioneer families took the same basic food supplies for their six-month trip. Typically, a family packed the following:

150 pounds of flour
40 pounds of sugar
40 pounds of coffee
40 pounds of smoked bacon
25 pounds of salt
5 pounds of baking soda
30-40 pounds of dried fruit

Pioneer diets might be supplemented by bags of cornmeal and rice. Many travelers carefully packed away other "necessities," such as yeast for baking, vinegar, molasses, even chocolate. Eggs could be taken but had to be protected in barrels of cornmeal or flour. Bacon would keep on the trip if it was kept out of the heat. Usually it was packed in a barrel of bran to keep the fat from melting down. Coffee was the most popular

Wagon-train travelers often stopped to rest and enjoy a hearty meal before continuing toward their western destination.

drink on the trail. Even children drank it. It was almost always boiled strong. This helped to mask the taste of western water, which was often bitter and loaded with alkali. Some horses that refused to drink western water would drink coffee instead. Cows were milked on the trail. The milk that was not drunk was placed in a pail, covered, and hung on the back of the wagon. After a day of shaking and jolting, the milk became butter. Buffalo and other game along the trail were generally plentiful. They provided the emigrants with a supply of fresh meat.

Family milk cows were often taken along on the western trip. Many wagon trains were followed by a herd of such cattle. Often a single herder was selected daily to keep track of about 30 head of cattle. Sometimes men with no families signed on with a wagon train as cattle herders. These bachelors became responsible for the train's entire herd.

The Portable Kitchen

Wagon-train travelers had to cook out on the trail. Their "kitchens" were the great outdoors. They cooked over open, well-drafted fire pits. Firewood was scarce along the western prairie trail. Cottonwood grew along river banks, but the emigrants were often far from flowing water. Buffalo chips—dried dung—soon became the common fuel on the prairie. Each day, children were sent out to collect the chips. And with millions of plains buffalo, there were plenty of chips!

Many pioneers brought along **dutch ovens,** sheet-iron stoves which could be used to cook bread and other trail foods. Preparing a meal on the trail was very hard, and there was the additional trouble of cooking at high altitudes on the plateaus and in the mountains. Sometimes it was hard even to bring water to a boil up in the mountains!

Handy Trail Guides

As more and more new Americans headed west along the Oregon and California trails, the demand for guidebooks increased. Some of these books were unreliable, though others were quite useful. One of the first was written in 1831 by Hall Jackson Kelley. Another early guidebook, entitled *An Emigrant Guide to Oregon and California,* was published by Lansford W. Hastings in 1845. These books gave travelers who were leaving for the west important information on all sorts of details about western trail travel. They described the landmarks to look for along the trail and gave information on distances. The books told travelers where to cross rivers, gave tips on how to stay healthy on the trail, and provided instructions on high-altitude cooking. There was also information on what weather to expect, how to take a wagon up a steep mountain, how to treat snakebites, and what to do to prevent boredom. Many travelers carried such books and memorized them from cover to cover.

The Route Followed by Thousands

Nearly all pioneers traveling west in the 1840s and 1850s, bound for Oregon and California, went along the same basic route. The eastern point of departure for the Oregon Trail was Independence, Missouri. Pioneer families and their wagons gathered there in the spring, anxious to begin their new lives out west. Most wagon trains left by April, after the spring thaws. Leaving at this time meant that the prairie grass of Kansas and Nebraska would be tall and plentiful. The emigrants' livestock needed the grass for food. The trains followed the route of the old Santa Fe Trail for about two days. Then, about 40 miles from Independence, a crude, handmade sign pointed the pioneers to the road to Oregon.

A month or so after leaving Independence, the train reached Fort Kearney on the south bank of the Platte River. By then the party had traveled about 400 miles. The Platte was usually a shallow river, but very wide and difficult to cross. Quicksand was a problem, and the river bottom was soft and shifting.

Along the route through Nebraska Territory, pioneers kept a careful eye out for landmarks to mark the distance along the trail. Natural rock formations with names such as Court House Rock, Chimney Rock and Scott's Bluff were a few of nature's signposts. Then the travelers arrived at a trading post called Fort Laramie, in present-day Wyoming. The emigrants had covered nearly one-third the distance of the trail.

Although called a "fort," Laramie was not originally a military outpost. (It was purchased by the U.S. Army in 1849.) It was owned during the 1840s by the American Fur Company and was one of the few stops along the trail where the pioneers could buy needed supplies. They could also receive expert help fixing their wagons at the fort. Here the travelers and their stock rested for several days. The pioneers naturally had an interest in any local news. They had questions about the local Indians, the best river crossings ahead, recent weather conditions, and stories of any recent cholera outbreaks.

Back on the Oregon Trail once again, the pioneers followed the North Platte and Sweetwater rivers and soon found themselves in mountain country. It was August and the emigrants frequently found snow along the mountain trail. Here a large formation, the turtle-shell-shaped Independence Rock, loomed ahead. Many a pioneer took the time to scratch his or her name on the massive rock. Mountain men and women had begun the practice before the Oregon Trail was so heavily traveled. Independence Rock served as a "register" for the emigrants. It was their way of "signing in" as some of the new westerners.

Independence Rock was a famous landmark for the pioneers.

At South Pass, the wagon train slipped through the **Continental Divide,** the point in the Rocky Mountains separating those rivers flowing east from those flowing west. In 1812, Robert Stuart was the first settler to see South Pass. Here some pioneers bound for Oregon took a different route. A shortcut named Sublette's Cutoff saved time and mileage for a wagon headed for Oregon. But taking the cutoff meant bypassing Fort Bridger, which was a needed stop for some weary travelers.

At Fort Bridger, emigrants had found their first opportunity to leave the Oregon Trail and set off south for California. Those who took this route skirted around the southern shore of the Great Salt Lake and took Hastings's Cutoff to the Humboldt River, then through the Sierra Nevada to California.

Those who stayed on the Oregon Trail journeyed north past Soda Springs, Idaho. Emigrants taking the shortcut drank the bubbly mineral waters here and found it tickled their noses. Up the road was Fort Hall, a trading post. It had been established in 1834 by a New England fur trader named Nathaniel Wyeth.

Remaining Oregon Trail travelers were soon given their second chance to go to California instead of Oregon. The trail forked west of the fort and headed southwest, again to the turnoff at the Humboldt River. At Fort Hall, the pioneers had successfully completed approximately two-thirds of their journey to Oregon.

Those determined to finish their trip in Oregon traveled northwest. Ahead was the Snake River, well named for its twisting course. The pioneers followed along the south side of the Snake for 250 miles. The commonly used crossing was 600 feet wide. It was made in very swift-moving water. Frequently, for safety, the emigrants chained their wagons together in a long line to make the crossing. Sometimes wagons were unloaded and the goods were rafted across the river. On other occasions wagons were taken apart and floated across the raging mountain river.

From the Snake River crossing, it was about 100 miles to Fort Boise. Another mountain range had to be conquered—the Blue Mountains—before the travelers could pass the Whitman Mission and then behold the welcome sight of Fort Walla Walla on the banks of the Columbia River. The long trip to Oregon was by then nearly over. All that stood between the seasoned pioneers and the rich farmland of the Willamette River valley was the Dalles, a stretch of river rapids along the Columbia River. With this last leg of their long, tiresome trip over, the pioneers walked triumphantly into Fort Vancouver, near the mouth of the Willamette River. The 2,000-mile trip from Independence, Missouri, was over. Usually, it was late October.

Pioneer families were often brought closer together through the experiences they shared on the trail.

The Daily Routine on the Trail

Traveling across the wilderness prairie could be an exciting experience. There were challenging river crossings, beautiful mountain scenery, unfamiliar animals to see and even an occasional American Indian riding by. But often the daily routine of trail travel was a little boring. Most wagon trains followed a regular schedule each day.

A day on the Oregon Trail began with gunshots. The night guards fired their rifles at 4:00 A.M., signaling to the rested pioneers that a new day had arrived. The sentinels had often tried to keep some fires going through the night. Fires were rekindled. Families roused in their wagons, dressing for the day. Animals outside the camp were brought together. Most of the livestock naturally stayed together through the nights for warmth and protection from the wolves.

Within an hour the oxen and mules were harnessed or yoked. The emigrants ate breakfast. Often they ate bacon, which they called **sowbelly,** and a type of pancake they called **slam-johns.** They then cleaned up their camp.

By 7:00 A.M. the wagon train was formed, ready to begin moving on. Often the wagon leader gave a shout of "Wagons ho!" and movement along the long wagon line began. Sometimes a wagon train stretched out a distance of between a half to three-quarters of a mile in length! Any wagon joining the line late went to the end. All wagons regularly rotated positions each day in the train, taking their turns in front.

As the wagon train snaked its way along the trail, everyone found his or her own activity to fight the boredom. Some knitted or walked along, talking to neighbors. Others rode horses. Children ran along, chasing each other out on the open plains. Older children played games. Sometimes dried buffalo chips were sailed like Frisbees. The youngest children—those who could not walk and keep up—often stayed in the wagons, playing with each other and hiding among the great pile of family goods brought along for the journey. Children also herded goats and other livestock alongside the wagon. Although the trip was often boring for adults, the trail was a highway of adventure for most of the children. After all, they were getting a break from many of their regular farm chores.

After four hours of travel—covering perhaps eight miles of ground—the wagons stopped for **nooning,** the midday break for the emigrants and their livestock. The oxen and mules all needed this important rest. Here the morning talk generally ended and work began. There was lunch to prepare and clothing to wash. The washing was usually done at a nearby river or stream. Some pioneers on the trail suffered from frequent back pains brought on by constantly bending over cooking fires and washboards.

There were other chores too. Livestock were turned out to feed. Travelers checked the leather harnesses for breaks and uneven wearing, and they examined the stock for sores or split hooves. Squeaky wagon wheels were greased. Scouts reported on the condition of the trail ahead. They told the others about any buffalo or Indians they had seen.

By 2:00 P.M. the train started up again for the longest stretch of the day. Many trains kept moving until late in the evening, often after dark. Sometimes trains did not stop until 10:00 P.M., but only if there was enough moonlight to do night chores. Out on the western prairies, the moon gave off enough bluish light on a clear night to allow people to do their chores. As often as not, however, a wagon train stopped around 5:00 or 6:00 P.M. and made camp.

Evening fires were lighted and the weary emigrants settled down from a day of travel. The night camp was then set up. The wagons were drawn into a circle and often chained together. Larger wagon trains divided into eight-wagon units, each called a **mess,** and formed individual circles. Often the heaviest meal of the day was eaten then. Perhaps fresh meat, such as buffalo steak or stewed prairie chicken, was cooked. After dinner, pioneers sometimes read their Bibles or even listened to a sermon if a preacher was part of the train. There might be music, as many pioneers brought along a fiddle or a harmonica. Several enjoyed singing together. Perhaps there was a quick dance or a one-person jig performance before the day was over. Soon the tired pioneers made their way to their beds. Most pioneers slept on the ground under their wagons. If unfriendly native Americans or others had been spotted that day, the livestock might be placed inside the wagon circle. Night guards or sentinels were posted and armed with shotguns instead of rifles. Guards often fell asleep on duty. When caught, they were punished, usually by being made to travel at the back of the wagon train.

At the end of a typical day the pioneers might lie on their mats thinking about what needed to be done the following day. They had worked hard. Their wagons were, perhaps, 12 to 15 miles closer to their dreams in Oregon and California.

Evenings offered tired travelers a chance to relax after a long day's journey.

A wagon-train accident was a sad and common sight along the trail.

Death on the Trail

The emigrants who went west on the Oregon Trail were usually strong and healthy. They understood many of the hardships and problems they had to face during the six-month trip. But death was a common experience along the Oregon Trail. Disease was a constant threat. Many of the diseases they feared, such as smallpox and measles, can be easily treated today. But at that time many people, both young and old, died of these and other dreaded illnesses.

One deadly disease was dysentery. Pioneers called it the **relax disease.** This illness brought on frequent attacks of diarrhea. Poor sanitation was one cause of the disease. Dysentery did not always kill, but it always caused a person to suffer greatly. Pioneers were immensely weakened by dysentery.

But the disease that the emigrants feared more than any other was cholera, a gastrointestinal illness.

Once a person had the disease, he or she died very quickly. Some pioneers became ill in the morning and died before the day was over. Few lasted longer than several days. Carried by bacteria, the disease caused its victims to dehydrate. Cholera victims went into shock shortly before they experienced the "black vomit," which meant approaching death. Cholera had come from Asia and spread through the United States during the 1830s and 1840s. It was feared by wagon-train travelers because it could move quickly through the group from one wagon to another. Those who died of the disease, or from any other trail disease, were hurriedly buried along the trail. Trail graves were dug deep and often covered with heavy rocks to keep wolves from digging up the bodies.

Accidents were fairly common along the Oregon Trail. River crossings witnessed frequent drownings. The majority of people at that time did not know how to swim. Falls along mountain trails brought death to some. Rambunctious children who stood on the tongues of moving wagons sometimes fell off, rolling under the heavy wagon wheels which crushed them to death.

Gunshot wounds were also common. Many of those who went west on the trail had rarely carried or fired a gun. People fell on their guns. Guns were accidentally discharged. A common mistake was made along the trail when men stuck handguns in their belts, causing the pistols to go off. Such a wound could prove very embarrassing.

Women died not only of disease but also during childbirth on the trail. Traveling was hard enough, but to be pregnant during much of the six-month trip was difficult indeed. Women often gave birth prematurely. Such early-birth babies did not usually survive.

Pioneers were killed by lightning, trampled by stampeding buffalo, poisoned by bad water, suffered heart attacks and heat stroke, and died of appendicitis or any number of other causes. Modern estimates put the toll of emigrant deaths on the Oregon Trail at around 34,000, or nearly 10 percent of those who attempted the western trip. That number works out to an average of 17 deaths for each mile of the Oregon Trail.

The Tragedy of the Donner Party

Poor planning and fighting between pioneers could also bring death on the trail. In the summer of 1846 a group of 89 emigrants, led by George Donner, left Missouri in May, later than the usual wagon train. The 20-wagon train was the scene of constant quarreling between the travelers. One party member even killed another. He and his family were exiled, or separated from the wagon train. When Donner's group reached Fort Bridger, they knew they were behind schedule and took Hastings's Cutoff. This was a very unreliable trail. They had no guide and got lost.

The group was stranded in late October by a huge snowstorm in what became known as Donner Pass in the Sierra Nevada. The snow drifted to depths of 40 feet. Still stranded in mid-December, the party was nearly out of supplies. A group of 15 volunteered to leave the group and go for help.

This group also ran out of supplies and turned to cannibalism to stay alive. They ate the flesh of four party members who had died. Two of their American Indian guides refused to eat human "meat." They were then killed by the others and eaten as well.

The other stranded Donner party was not rescued until February 19, 1847. Many of them had died.

This group had engaged in cannibalism also. Those still alive told stories of how they passed pieces of meat around the surviving group so they would not know if they were eating the flesh of their dead relatives. Fewer than half of the original Donner party—a total of 45—survived the ordeal.

Survivors of the Donner Party tragedy endured severe winter conditions and starvation throughout their ordeal.

Native Americans Along the Trail

Along much of the Oregon Trail, pioneers found themselves in the neighborhood of native Americans. The trail passed through the lands of many nations, or tribes, on both sides of the Rocky Mountains. They called the trail the "Big Medicine Path." East of the Rockies were mostly plains tribes: the Sioux, Pawnee, Cheyenne, Crow, Blackfoot, Arapaho, Kiowa and Kansas. On the western side of the mountains, the Nez Perce, Bannock, Paiute, Yakima, Cayuse, Gosiute and the Shoshone roamed.

On the whole, travelers on the Oregon Trail were not bothered by these native Americans. Often Indians could be seen in the distance, watching as the long wagon trains slowly passed. Indian attacks on moving or encamped wagon trains were very rare.

Some tribes—such as the Crow and Blackfoot—did gain reputations as marauders. They did not want the settlers to cross their hunting grounds and violate their ancestral lands. Occasionally, members of those and other tribes caught unfortunate stragglers along the trail. These captives were often scalped or tortured to death.

But few emigrants ever saw a native American in war paint. The more common scene was that of trade between the settlers and the Indians. Sometimes Indians were seen along the trail, looking for handouts of food, tobacco or whiskey. Pioneers often traded guns for horses. And sometimes that same horse was spirited out of the wagon train's encampment that night by its original native American owner.

Horse stealing by the Indians was fairly common along the trail. The Pawnees had, perhaps, the worst reputation among settlers for stealing not just horses but anything they could get their hands on. More than a few pioneers arose at dawn to find everything from guns to horses to clothing to cows to the very blankets they had slept with the night before gone.

Some American Indians collected "tolls" from the wagon trains. They collected money for helping the emigrants raft their wagons across western rivers. Such a service might cost a pioneer family $3.00.

In many Hollywood movies, native Americans are shown riding their war ponies around a circle of pioneer wagons. This scene rarely happened on the Oregon Trail. During the 1840s and 1850s, 250,000 settlers traveled the Big Medicine Path. Of that number, only 362 pioneers on the trail were killed by native Americans. Whites killed an estimated 425 Indians.

Pioneers were happy to trade with the native Americans and pay them for their helpful services along the trail.

The End of the Trail

Until the outbreak of the Civil War, the Oregon and California trails saw heavy traffic. But during the war years (1861-1865), few settlers traveled west. The trail became quiet and deserted—except for the Pony Express, which ran from April 3, 1860, to October 24, 1861. That short-lived mail service followed most of the Oregon Trail. Many men stayed back east to serve in the Northern or Southern armies. After the war, emigration returned to the Oregon Trail. People wanted once again to go west to find new lives for themselves. But the trail never again saw the numbers of pioneers and wagons that had passed along its rivers and landmarks during the 1840s and 1850s. The completion of the transcontinental railroad in May 1869 helped to make the Oregon Trail almost unnecessary for cross-country travel. But for years to come, wagons could still be seen along the trail. Even as late as 1895, wagons were moving along the ancient

The Pony Express employed fearless young riders to travel on speedy horses through dangerous conditions along the Oregon Trail.

road, passing along sections of the trail where an earlier generation's wheels had carved ruts a foot deep into solid rock. But by that time, the great American adventure of the Oregon Trail was the subject of old diaries and fading memories.

★

For Further Reading

Catrow, David. *The Story of the Oregon Trail.* Chicago: Childrens Press, 1984.

Fisher, Leonard Ever. *The Oregon Trail.* New York: Holiday House, 1990.

Gildemeister, Jerry. *A Letter Home.* Union, OR: Bear Wallow Publishers, 1987.

Noonan, Jon. *Lewis and Clark.* New York: Crestwood House, 1993.

Santrey, Laurence. *The Oregon Trail.* Mahwah, NJ: Troll Associates, 1985.

Glossary

Astoria—Fur-trapping and trading post on the Columbia River in Oregon. It was founded in 1811 for John Jacob Astor and his Pacific Fur Company, by Robert Stuart.

Continental Divide—A ridge running from north to south in the Rocky Mountains, which separates rivers and streams flowing to the Pacific from those flowing toward the Atlantic.

dutch oven—A metal box that opens in front and is often used for roasting meat on an open fire.

great migration—The journey by 1,000 pioneers in 1843. They traveled on the Oregon Trail, the largest number to that date. Many of them traveled in a large train of 120 wagons.

linseed oil—A yellowish oil made by pressing the seed of flax.

mess—An eight-wagon unit of a longer wagon train. Such wagons would circle together at night, and the travelers would eat meals together.

mountain man—Fur trapper who lived in the western areas, especially the Rocky Mountains. Most mountain people were active in the years from 1810 to 1840.

nooning—The midday break for western pioneer wagon trains on the Oregon and California trails.

Oregon Country—The western lands of modern-day Oregon and Washington states.

Oregon Trail—Wagon road which ran from St. Joseph, Missouri, to the Oregon Country. The route followed the North Platte River in Nebraska, the Snake River in Idaho and the Columbia River in Oregon. It crossed the Rockies at South Pass. Thousands of pioneer families used the trail in the 1830s, 1840s and 1850s.

prairie schooner—A western wagon with white canvas covers that resemble a ship's sails.

relax disease—Dysentery; the main symptom is extreme diarrhea.

rendezvous—An event held in the summer at the end of the trapping season. A rendezvous was a place where fur trappers could sell their pelts (hides) to traders. Rendezvous were held in the Rocky Mountains between 1824 and 1840.

slam-johns—Pioneer pancakes.

South Pass—Break located in the Rocky Mountains. It was used by western pioneers on the Oregon and California trails.

sowbelly—A type of bacon eaten by wagon-train travelers.

Index